# This book belongs to:

Joshua C. Corrales

# MESSAGE TO PARENTS

This book is perfect for parents and children to read aloud together. First read the story to your child. When you read it again  run your finger under each line, stopping at each picture for your child to "read." Help your child to figure out the picture. If your child makes a mistake, be encouraging as you say the right word. Point out the written word beneath each picture in the margin on the page. Soon your child will be "reading" aloud with you, and at the same time learning the symbols that stand for words.

EDITED BY
DEBORAH SHINE

DESIGN BY
CANARD DESIGN, INC.

# Move Over, Roger

## A Read Along With Me Book

By Cindy West

Illustrated by Olivia Cole

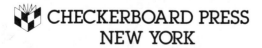 CHECKERBOARD PRESS
NEW YORK

Roger

house

Sam

Jenny

sun

Early one summer morning

ran around the  , barking so

loudly he woke up  and

"Oh,  ," groaned

sleepily.  "Just because we're

moving, it doesn't mean we

have to get up with the  ."

car

Rags

sofa

After breakfast, everyone climbed into the . The cat  sat on 's lap, feeling sort of sad. She was going to miss the old  and the cozy she used to sleep on.

**Roger**

**Rags**

**men**

**sofa**

When they reached their new home,  bounded out of the  , eager to roll in the grass.  perked up when she saw the moving  carrying in her old  ! She jumped onto it and curled up for a nap.

Big, clumsy  jumped on too!

he moving  were so

urprised, they dropped the .

"Get off that !" yelled

it  opened one eye.

he liked it when  got into

ouble. "If he gets into more

ouble, they'll like me better,"

he thought to herself.

Everyone worked very hard

inpacking the .

Father

boxes

Sam

Jenny

can

brushes

fence

After lunch,  and  got

a  of paint and two ,

and began painting the .

Suddenly  had a

mischievous idea. She raced

over and bit  on the tail!

"Yeow!" he howled, heading

raight for the . "Watch out!"

shouted, grabbing the paint

just in time. But 's tail

ipped into the paint.

Rags

Roger

"Mee-oow!" screeched ,

and raced into the , painting

bright red stripe on the floor!

"!" scolded . "You've

got to behave!"  washed

's tail with  and water.

"I hate water!" groaned .

he was so angry, she ran out and

moped under the picnic .

"Hmm," thought . "I know

ow to get  in trouble."

ugged the tablecloth off the

 and tossed it onto !

Father

Jenny

soap

table

Roger

Roger

table

Sam

house

Jenny

"Woof! Why is it so dark?"

barked and ran past the .

"Help!"  yelled. "This

has a ghost!"

"Oh, that's  !"  laughe

"Uh-oh," 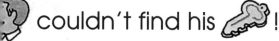 groaned. "A

storm's coming. We'd all better

get inside." But the wind had

slammed the door shut – and

 couldn't find his !

**Father**

**key**

**Mother**

**key**

**Roger**

**pots**

**pans**

**plates**

"Don't worry," said  .

"I know I packed an extra

somewhere. Everyone can help

look for it."

 sniffed around the

and  and  .

**dish**

**Jenny**

When he found his own ,

he got so excited, he picked it up

and brought it to .

, it's not dinnertime yet,"

she scolded. "Go back and

keep looking for the ."

But 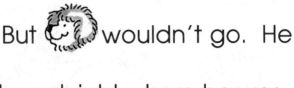 wouldn't go. He

stayed right where he was,

barking and pointing at his

Finally  looked inside the

– and saw the  !

"  found the  !"

shouted  .

She opened the front  and

everyone rushed into the  .

 was the first one through th

 ! She couldn't wait to get

away from all that pouring water!

 got a towel and dried off

 and  . Then  lit a

ire in the fireplace.

 was so happy to be warm

and dry, she snuggled next to  .

**key**

**Rags**

**Roger**

**house**

"How did you ever find that ?" 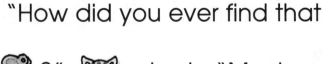 asked. "Maybe you're smarter than I thought."

 nodded modestly. "And I think I found a patch of catnip, too, " he said.

Catnip!  began purring loudly. "I think I <u>am</u> going to like this new . I even like , too – sometimes."

 smiled proudly.  Soon

 and  fell asleep, snug

and warm in their new home.

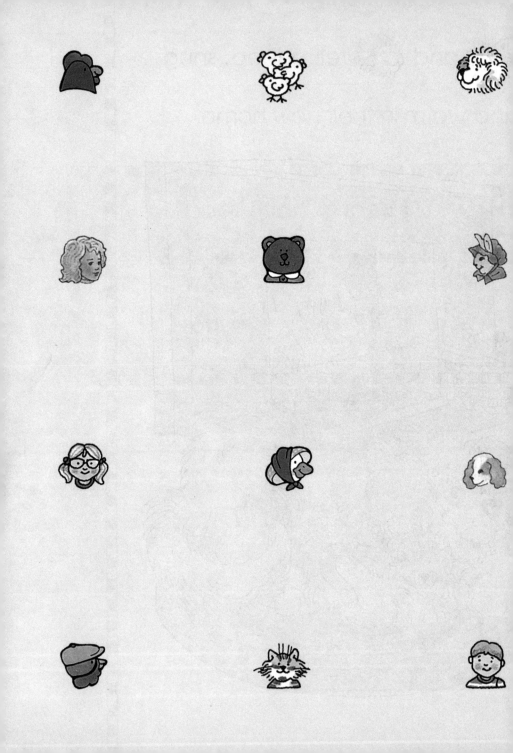